Jingle Bells

HOW THE
HOLIDAY CLASSIC
CAME TO BE

Written by
John Harris

Illustrated by
Adam Gustavson

Jingle Bells

HOW THE HOLIDAY CLASSIC CAME TO BE

PEACHTREE
ATLANTA

Hot.

JAMES LORD PIERPONT felt his starched shirt sticking to his back. How could it be this hot in November? Christmas was only a month away, but here in Savannah, it was still sweltering.

As he walked up the aisle of his church, broken glass crunched beneath his boot. He spotted a brick on a nearby pew.

"Not again," he sighed. "Lillie, be careful."

"Why would anyone break our windows?" his daughter asked.

"Well, some people don't like our church because we don't believe in slavery," Mr. Pierpont said. "Someone is probably angry because our congregation has four members who once were slaves. Four members who are much more likely to go to heaven than the person who threw that brick, I might add."

Lillie Knelt to help her father clean up the broken glass. A sticky breeze blew through the broken window.

"It's so hot here," said Mr. Pierpont. "At this time of year in Boston, it would already be cold and crisp. And one morning you would wake up and the ground would be covered with snow."

"What's snow like, exactly?" asked Lillie.

Mr. Pierpont shook his head sadly. His own child had never seen snow...

"Well, the air feels sharp," he told her. "You can see your breath. There's nothing in the world like sitting in a snug little sleigh beside a friend, watching the snow-covered world race by. You'd have a nice warm brick at your feet, not one crashing through—"

The door opened, startling them both.

"Why, Mr. Pierpont. I had no idea you would be here."

A stately woman stood in the doorway. Behind her, almost hidden from view, was a little girl with deep brown skin.

Pierpont smiled. He admired this woman. Four years earlier, she had taken this child into her home.

"Good afternoon, Mrs. FitzHugh…Miss Esther. Take care not to step on the broken glass."

"What happened, Mr. Pierpont?" Mrs. FitzHugh asked.

"Another brick through a window, I'm afraid."

"Oh my," she said. "I don't understand how some people can be so mean-spirited, especially at this time of year."

Mr. Pierpont sighed and turned to Esther. "I like the flower in your hat," he said with a wink. "Just like someone else's."

Esther gave him a shy smile.

"I Hope we're not interrupting," said Mrs. FitzHugh. "We're here to pick up the flower vases."

Pierpont seemed puzzled.

"For the Thanksgiving concert. Or have you decided to cancel it because of the—" She glanced toward the brick on the pew.

"Please, Mr. Pierpont, we must have our concert," said Esther in a small voice. "We always enjoy singing your new song."

"I suppose I've been too worried to start working on it yet," said Mr. Pierpont. "Anyway, it's much too hot to think about the winter holidays." He stared out the window, lost in thought.

"Esther," he said finally. "Have you ever ridden in a sleigh? Or heard the sound of sleigh bells?"

The little girl shook her head.

"I don't think Lillie has either." His eyes lit up. "Just a minute."

Mr. Pierpont climbed the stairs to the balcony, where the church's pipe organ stood. He sat down and tapped a key three times. *Plink-plink-plink*. Then he did it again. "Sleigh bells sound a bit like that." He sang along.

"Here we go, here we go..."

Mrs. FitzHugh looked up at the balcony. "So musical," she called. "Jingling bells, riding in a sleigh. What fun that must be!"

Mr. Pierpont played the three notes again. "It is fun… *Here we go, jingling bells…*" He paused, then repeated the notes. *"Jingle bells, jingle bells…* That's what they sound like."

"Lovely," said Mrs. FitzHugh. "Lillie, could you help us find those vases? I think your father has work to do."

Mr. Pierpont played three notes, this time a little higher. What had Mrs. FitzHugh said?

"Oh what fun..."

Then he put the phrases together. *Jingle bells, jingle bells... Oh what fun, oh what fun...* He smiled to himself. Perhaps this was the beginning of the song he was looking for. *What we all need right now,* he thought, *is something to lift our spirits.*

James Lord Pierpont got out some paper and a pen.

$\mathcal{L}$ater that week, Mrs. FitzHugh and a friend dropped by the church during choir practice.

"I'll be right back," Mr. Pierpont told the children. "Behave while I speak with these ladies."

"You said you needed something?" asked Mrs. FitzHugh.

"I'm going to need blossoms for the concert!" Mr. Pierpont exclaimed. "Lots of them. White blossoms. Where can we find them?"

"By tomorrow?" said Mrs. FitzHugh. "I'm not sure that's possible."

There was a pause.

"Is something wrong with my hat, Mr. Pierpont?"

Mr. Pierpont smiled.

"Your hat, Mrs. FitzHugh, has given me another idea."

On the night of the concert, the church was filled. Even with the windows and the front door open, ladies fanned themselves and men's starched collars wilted in the heat.

At exactly 7:30, Mr. Pierpont strode down the aisle and faced his expectant audience.

"Every year at this time," he said, his voice carrying to the back of the church, "our children help us welcome the holiday season by performing a new song. Although we have all been disheartened by recent events, we think we've found a way to raise our spirits. Despite the heat, we'll try to help you experience the kind of winter we don't have here in Savannah. I hope you'll join us in singing 'One Horse Open Sleigh'."

The congregation grew quiet, waiting for the music to begin. From somewhere outside the church, they heard a faint jingling. The sound grew louder and louder, and people turned around in their seats, trying to see what was happening. Two little girls in choir robes entered the church, shaking strands of bells.

A murmur went around the room.

"How adorable!"

"Aren't they beautiful?"

Mrs. FitzHugh raised her hand to her mouth. Her little Esther looked so happy!

The girls reached the front of the church and slowly turned to face the congregation. Eight other children, each one holding a small bag, filed in and took their places behind them.

From the organ loft, Mr. Pierpont called down to the congregation. "This is the chorus of our new song. You'll only have to hear it once before you know how it goes." He played several notes by way of introduction, and the children began to sing:

Jingle bells,
Jingle bells,
Jingle all the way.
Oh, what fun it is to ride
In a one horse open sleigh.

Still shaking the bells, the children launched into the first verse:

Dashing through the snow,
In a one horse open sleigh...

As the children finished the song, they opened their bags and threw handfuls of white feathers up into the air, as high as they could. The congregation burst into applause.

"Thank you so much," said Mr. Pierpont when the commotion finally died down. "Feathers aren't snow," he said. "But they're the best we could do. And I'm glad you enjoyed our new song. Let's hope it goes out the doors and windows of our church—even through that broken window—and reaches the whole world!"

And James Lord Pierpont was right: it did.

A Note from the Author

I WROTE THIS STORY as a result of a visit to Savannah, Georgia. I was wandering around that beautiful city and came upon the historical marker saying that "Jingle Bells" had been written in Savannah by one James L. Pierpont. Now this, I thought, is interesting—such a song, in such a place! A story was begging to be written.

I did a little investigating and discovered that there are at least two versions of what happened. Some people claim that James Lord Pierpont, a prolific song-writer, wrote "Jingle Bells" in Medford, Massachusetts (he was born in Boston); others say Mr. Pierpont wrote it in Savannah, where he was serving as the music director at the Unitarian Church on Oglethorpe Square.

I side with the second group, obviously, and most other people do too. But wherever it may have been written, it was probably composed in the 1850s,

James Lord Pierpont

Sheet music for "Jingle Bells" (originally titled "One Horse Open Sleigh") deposited at the Library of Congress on September 16, 1857

because Mr. Pierpont copyrighted the song in 1857. This places its composition shortly before the Civil War.

If "Jingle Bells" was written in the South by a Unitarian from the North (the Unitarians were pretty staunch Abolitionists), if James Lord Pierpont had a young daughter named Lillie (he did), and if Savannah was experiencing a heat wave at Thanksgiving (which is when some people think Mr. Pierpont wrote the song).... In my mind, one "if" led to another, and this book is the result.

I'm not a historian and don't claim to be one. The nice people at the Unitarian church in Savannah showed me around and answered questions, and I hope they don't mind that I took a few liberties with the stories I heard. All I've tried to do, really, is remind the reader that a small and unexpected chain of events can provide the inspiration for something much bigger—in this case, a song that the whole world knows and loves.

This historic marker is located near Troup Square in Savannah, Georgia, across the street from the Unitarian Church

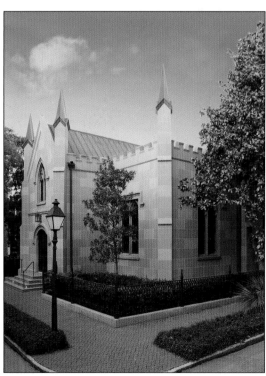

The Unitarian Universalist Church of Savannah

For Janice and Patrick
—*J. H.*

For my family
—*A. G.*

Ω

Published by
PEACHTREE PUBLISHERS
1700 Chattahoochee Avenue
Atlanta, Georgia 30318-2112
www.peachtree-online.com

Text © 2011 by John Harris
Illustrations © 2011 by Adam Gustavson
Photograph of the historical marker on page 31 © 2011 Kerry Shay.
Photograph of the Unitarian Universalist Church of Savannah on page 31 © 2011 Wayne C. Moore.
Photograph of James Lord Pierpont and reproductions of the sheet music for "One Horse Open Sleigh"
on page 30 are courtesy of the Library of Congress.

Design and composition by Janice Shay

Illustrations rendered in oil on prepared 100% cotton archival watercolor paper; titles
typeset in Umbrella Type's Phaeton by Kevin Cornell and Randy Jones; text typeset in
International Typeface Corporation's Caxton Book by Leslie Usherwood

Printed in March 2011 by Imago in Singapore
10 9 8 7 6 5 4 3 2 1
First Edition

Library of Congress Cataloging-in-Publication Data

Harris, John, 1950 July 7-
 Jingle bells : how the holiday classic came to be/ written by John Harris ; illustrated by Adam Gustavson.
    p. cm.
 Summary: Tells the story of how, in Savannah, Georgia, in 1857 James Lord Pierpont sat down to write
a song for his congregation's Thanksgiving program and, homesick for the cold New England weather
he remembered, came up with an enduring classic.
 ISBN 978-1-56145-590-4, 1-56145-590-3
 1. Pierpont, James, 1822-1893. Jingle bells—Juvenile fiction. [1. Pierpont, James, 1822-1893.
Jingle bells—Fiction.] I. Gustavson, Adam, ill. II. Title.
 PZ7.H7373Ji 2011
—[E]—dc22
                            2010052274